*For Wendy,*
*my editor and friend*

Copyright © 2000 by Bob Graham
The characters in this book have appeared in the
magazine *Pomme d'Api* published by Bayard Presse, France, in 1997.

First U.S. edition 2000

Library of Congress Cataloging-in-Publication Data

Graham, Bob.
Max / Bob Graham.—1st ed.
p.   cm.
Summary: Max, the young son of superheroes, is a late bloomer when it comes to flying,
until he is inspired by the plight of a falling baby bird.
ISBN 0-7636-1138-7
[1. Heroes—Fiction.  2. Flight—Fiction.]
I. Title.
PZ7.G751667 Max 2000        [E]—dc21    99-043704

2 4 6 8 10 9 7 5 3 1

Printed in Hong Kong

This book was typeset in Stempel Schneidler Medium.
The illustrations were done in ink and watercolor.

Candlewick Press
2067 Massachusetts Avenue
Cambridge, Massachusetts 02140

# MAX

## BOB GRAHAM

CANDLEWICK PRESS
CAMBRIDGE, MASSACHUSETTS

Morning arrived on a
street like any other street,
in a town like any other town.

In a house the color of
the sun and the shape
of a lightning bolt, a baby
woke up in his crib.

Not just any baby.
He was a superbaby—
son of superheroes
Captain Lightning and
Madam Thunderbolt.

Imagine him behind those
yellow walls, his fingers
curling and his feet kicking.

His name was . . .

# Max.

His parents—legendary catchers of thieves and bullies—
loved Max dearly.

"You can walk already," said Max's dad,

"and you can talk already,

"and I think that you'll soon be . . .

"flying like a bird!"

"He'll be a superhero, just like us!" said his grandma.

"But first he'll need to fly!" said his grandad.

Although they bounced him and bumped him, and threw him like a feather on the wind . . .

Max did not fly. He just floated
gently back to Earth.

Max grew, as superbabies do. But still he didn't fly.

"Just hover a little," said Madam Thunderbolt.

"Every superhero needs to hover and hurtle and swoop."

"Well, maybe sometime soon," she added.

At home, Max and Phantom the dog played on the floor.

"Come on up and join me with the parakeet!" said his dad.

"I can't," said Max. "I want to play with Phantom."

"He walked and talked so early," said Captain Lightning, "I can't understand why he doesn't fly."

"When I was his age," said his grandad, "I got into trouble for leaving fingerprints on the ceiling lamp."

By the time he went to school,
Max was not a flying superhero,
but just an ordinary boy with
a cape and a mask . . .

which were no help to him at all in the schoolyard.

"Why don't you do tough things like your mom and dad?"

"And why do you dress in those funny clothes?" asked Aaron.

"Why don't you fly?" asked Daisy.

Max just shrugged.

The sun rose one morning with the world-famous superheroes
deep in dreams of yesterday's exploits.

Grandma and Grandad dreamed of heroic past deeds.
Phantom dreamed of rabbits.

Who could know that
a baby bird was about
to fall from its nest?

Max knew.
Max saw it from
his open window.
This bird was
not ready to fly.

He ran to the stairs,

and took
them three
at a time.

He reached
the front door,

and pulled
it open.

The baby bird fell.
Max flew to save it.

Max flew the baby bird back to its nest.
"You be careful up there, Max," called Captain Lightning.
Madam Thunderbolt swelled with pride.

In the weeks that followed, Max could be seen hovering
like a summer dragonfly above the school gates.

Try as she might, Miss Honeyset couldn't keep
him firmly in his seat in class.

At lunchtime in the schoolyard,
to his friends he was still
plain and ordinary "Max" . . .

Well, not *quite* ordinary.
But then, as Aaron said,
"Everyone's different
in *some* way, aren't they?"

Now that Max can fly,
will he become a superhero
like his legendary parents?

Will he hurtle and swoop
to catch thieves, crooks,
and bullies?

"Not important," said Madam Thunderbolt.
"Let's call him a small hero, a small hero doing quiet deeds.
The world needs more of those."

Max wished his mom wouldn't hug him in public.

Now on Sundays, after their week's work is finished,
Captain Lightning, Madam Thunderbolt, and Max
ride high in the warm air over the town.

"Can we go up into the jet stream?" asks Max.
"Whenever you're ready, Max," answer the legendary
superheroes Captain Lightning and Madam Thunderbolt.